WIND POWER!

Based on the teleplay "Epic Sail" by Dustin Ferrer
Adapted by Frank Berrios • Illustrated by Benjamin Burch

 A GOLDEN BOOK • NEW YORK

randomhousekids.com
T#: 450898
ISBN 978-1-101-93682-5
Printed in the United States of America
10 9 8 7 6 5 4 3

It was a hot, sunny day, and Blaze and his buddies were ready to cool off! They went down to the river to catch a cool breeze on a sailboat.

"This boat is amazing!" said Gabby.

"Yeah, Blaze! How do you make it go so fast?" asked Stripes.

"The sailboat moves fast because it's powered by the wind," explained Blaze. "Wind has the power to push things!"

"When wind blows against the sail, it pushes our boat forward through the water," said Blaze. "That's wind power!"

"I like it!" growled Stripes as the boat sliced across the ocean.

Nearby, Crusher and Pickle were having trouble with their boat.

"Oops," said Pickle as the sail fell on top of his pal, Crusher.

"Ahoy, Crusher! You need some help?" shouted Blaze.

"Ha! I don't need help," replied Crusher. "Besides, my boat is way faster than yours."

"I don't know, Crusher," said Stripes. "Our boat is pretty fast."

"Oh, yeah? Then let's have a race!" said Crusher.

"Okay, racers," said Gabby. "On your marks, get set, SAIL!"

With a gust of wind, Blaze and his friends zipped across the water. But Crusher's boat didn't go anywhere.

"Uh-oh, Crusher. I think you're losing," said Pickle.

"Well, looks like there's only one thing I can do to win this race," Crusher announced. *"Cheat."*

"I'm going to make something to knock Blaze's boat right out of my way!" giggled Crusher. "I'll build . . . a Wild Wavemaker!" With the press of a button, the wavemaker began to hum, and the water got rough and choppy.

"Oh, my," said Pickle. "Those are some big waves."

"That ought to stop Blaze," added Crusher.

"Where'd all these waves come from?" asked Blaze as his boat began to rock back and forth.

"It's Crusher!" exclaimed Gabby, pointing at their boat. "He's making them!"

The waves grew so big and rough, they pushed Blaze's boat up onto a beach!

"Whoa. We've landed on a tropical island," observed Blaze.

"And look! Our sailboat is broken!" exclaimed Stripes.

"Our boat is missing some really important pieces," added AJ. "The mast, the mainsheet, and the sail are gone!"

"Without those pieces, we can't use wind power!" said Gabby.

"And that means we can't sail home!" said Stripes.

"Hey, Gabby, if we find the missing parts, can you fix our sailboat?" asked Blaze.

"You bet I can!" replied Gabby. "I can fix anything!"

"Great!" Blaze said. "Then let's go find them!"

Meanwhile, Crusher and Pickle had washed up onto another part of the island.

"Look! Our sailboat is broken!" said Pickle. "But that's okay. You and me, we'll just work together and fix it."

"Oh, all right," replied Crusher. "But let's hurry—I want to sail away before Blaze so we can get home first!"

On the other side of the island, AJ, Blaze, and Stripes found the mast from their boat.

"There it is!" said AJ. "It's on that cliff!"

"How are we gonna get there without falling into that goo?" Blaze wondered aloud.

"I can do it!" said Stripes. But the rocks were too far apart for Stripes to jump. Then Blaze had a better idea!

"Stripes, you can use wind power!" suggested Blaze. "If you wait until the wind is blowing, it can push you and help you jump farther!"

Blaze and his friends found the mainsheet—just as a monkey ran off with it!

"I'll catch him!" Blaze said.

Vroom! Blaze used his rocket boosters to catch the silly monkey.

After getting the mainsheet back, Blaze and his friends needed one more piece to fix their boat.

"Look! There's our sail!" yelled Stripes.

"It's blowing away!" said Blaze. "C'mon! We're going to need everyone's help!"

Meanwhile, when Crusher saw the sail float by, he got an idea.

"We're going to take that sail and use it for our boat!" he told Pickle.

"Oh, no!" said Stripes. "Crusher is trying to take our sail!"

"We can get to the sail super fast if we use wind power!" replied Blaze. "Let's build a kite so we can fly up and get it!" With that, he changed into a huge glider. "I'm a kite-flying monster machine!"

Using wind power, Blaze and AJ soared to the top of the mountain.

"We've got the sail!" said Blaze. "Let's put it back on our boat so we all can go home!"

"Our boat is fixed!" said Gabby.

"Now we can sail back to Axle City!" cheered Stripes.

"Guess what, slowpokes. I fixed my sailboat first!" Crusher teased—just as his boat began to sink! Blaze and Stripes raced to the rescue.

"Here, grab one of these!" Blaze said, and he threw a couple of life preservers to the splashing trucks.

"Hooray! Blaze saved us!" cheered Pickle.

"Well, at least I can finally relax," grumbled Crusher, snuggling into his life preserver. "Yup, from here on out, it's smooth sailing."

Suddenly, a little crab gave Crusher a pinch!

"Ow-ow-ow!" yelped the blue truck.

Blaze and his friends sailed back to Axle City for more adventures!